W9-BNA-814

Christmas in Mouseland

The Show Must Go On

Published by Pleasant Company Publications
© 2003 Helen Craig Limited and Katharine Holabird
Based on the text by Katharine Holabird and the illustrations by Helen Craig
From the script by Mellie Buse

The Angelina Ballerina name and character and the dancing Angelina logo are trademarks of HIT
Entertainment PLC, Katharine Holabird, and Helen Craig. ANGELINA is registered in the U.K. and Japan.
The dancing Angelina logo is registered in the U.K.

All rights reserved. No part of this book may be used or reproduced in any manner whatsoever without
written permission except in the case of brief quotations embodied in critical articles and reviews.
For information, address: Book Editor, Pleasant Company Publications,
8400 Fairway Place, P.O. Box 620998, Middleton, Wisconsin 53562.

Visit our Web site at www.americangirl.com and
Angelina's very own site at www.angelinaballerina.com

Printed in the United States of America

03 04 05 06 07 08 09 10 NGS 10 9 8 7 6 5 4 3 2 1

Angelina™
Ballerina

Christmas in Mouseland

The Show Must Go On

PLEASANT
COMPANY
PUBLICATIONS™

Angelina held up a beautiful ballgown as she danced before
the mirror.

"Careful, dear!" said Mrs. Mouseling, who was busy
sewing costumes for Miss Lilly's ballet class. The class was
putting on a special Christmas performance of *Cinderella
Mouse* for Queen Seraphina of Mouseland.

As Angelina twirled, the gown swirled gracefully around her. "I can't wait to play the part of Cinderella Mouse!" she said excitedly.

"Don't forget that you have to audition for the part first," Mr. Mouseling reminded Angelina as he tugged at the Christmas tree in the corner of the room.

But Angelina was so busy dreaming about the ballet that she scarcely heard her father.

On the way to ballet class, Angelina and her best friend, Alice, spotted a poster for the *Cinderella Mouse* ballet.

"Alice, you do think I'll get the part, don't you?" Angelina asked hopefully.

"Father Christmas would choose you!" said little cousin Henry, who was very excited about Christmas. He carried his knit stocking as he skipped along the snowy sidewalk.

When the mouselings reached the toy shop window, they pressed their noses against the glass and peered inside.

"Alice, look at the toy theater!" gasped Angelina. "It's wonderful!" Angelina could almost imagine herself dancing on the tiny stage. She gazed through the window long after the other mouselings had run on ahead.

At ballet class, Miss Lilly showed Henry how to dance the part of the little beetle who turns into a coachmouse.

"Now crouch down, Henry, then leap up tall!" said Miss Lilly, spreading her arms into the air.

But Henry couldn't concentrate. "Miss Lilly, does Father Christmas ring the doorbell?" he asked, and "What if Father Christmas gets stuck in my chimney?"

Mr. Operatski, the famous director who was helping Miss Lilly with the ballet, leaped out of his chair. "This beetle will need a lot of work, Miss Lilly!" he grumbled.

"Henry will do fine," Miss Lilly said kindly. "And wait till you see his cousin, Angelina!"

Now it was Angelina's turn to dance. She leaped and twirled across the floor and finished in a beautiful pose.

"Charming!" said Mr. Operatski. "You certainly are the best mouseling to dance the part of Cinderella Mouse."

"But now," Mr. Operatski continued, "let's see who is the best mouseling to SING the part! The Queen loves music."

Angelina's heart fell in her chest. She didn't like singing in front of everyone. She felt much too nervous.

Angelina took a deep breath and opened her mouth. "La-la-la-la . . ." she began. Suddenly, Angelina's voice squeaked. Priscilla Pinkpaws quickly covered her ears.

"Humph!" said Mr. Operatski. "Not quite the angel I had in mind. Angelina, you will play the Wicked Stepmouse!"

Angelina was terribly disappointed. She would not play the part of Cinderella Mouse. That part had been given to Priscilla.

Miss Lilly came to visit Angelina that afternoon. "There are many ways of being a star," Miss Lilly said gently. She set the Wicked Stepmouse's crown on Angelina's head. "You will be a marvelous Wicked Stepmouse."

Angelina practiced making wicked faces in the mirror, but she couldn't stop dreaming about playing Cinderella Mouse. Then Angelina had an idea . . .

At rehearsal the next day, Angelina practiced the part of the Wicked Stepmouse. But instead of singing wickedly, Angelina sang in her sweetest voice. And instead of dancing big, bold steps, she danced gracefully.

Then, when Priscilla began her Cinderella dance, Angelina fell in beside her, performing the steps perfectly. Angelina danced her heart out.

"Stop!" said Mr. Operatski. "Angelina, did I ask to see you dance?"

"I'm sorry," said Angelina in a small, sweet voice. "I just couldn't help myself. This is my best dance!"

Mr. Operatski threw his arms into the air. "If Angelina is your best dancer," he said to Miss Lilly, "why can't she dance the part of the Wicked Stepmouse?"

Miss Lilly scolded Angelina. "Stop trying to be Cinderella," said Miss Lilly. "You are the Wicked Stepmouse."

"But it should never have turned out like this!" said Angelina.

"Priscilla is playing Cinderella," Miss Lilly said firmly. "Nothing will change that, and the show must go on."

"Then it will have to go on without ME!" said Angelina as she burst into tears and rushed offstage. She buried her face in her hands and cried miserably.

The next morning, Angelina heard laughter from outside her bedroom window. She saw Priscilla and her sister, Penelope, walking past the front gate. "Thank goodness Miss Lilly's going to play the Wicked Stepmouse," Priscilla was saying. "Angelina was hopeless!"

Angelina sighed and sank down beside the window, feeling very sorry for herself.

Mrs. Mouseling knocked gently on Angelina's bedroom door and asked, "Are you coming to breakfast, dear?"

"No," said Angelina sadly. "I don't have to get to the theater now that I'm not in the show anymore."

But a little while later, Angelina came downstairs and slipped into her winter coat. "I'm going for a walk," she told her mother.

On the street outside, Angelina ran into her friend Sammy.
He was pulling a toboggan behind him. "Want to race the
Pinkpaws twins down Cheddar Hill?" Sammy asked
Angelina.

Soon the toboggans were perched high atop the hill. As they slid forward, Angelina crouched low. Her toboggan gained speed, and Angelina and Sammy took the lead.

Just then, Angelina saw two figures walking along the sidewalk below. It was Miss Lilly and Mr. Operatski! Angelina tried to turn the toboggan, but it was too late. The mouselings crashed right into Miss Lilly.

"Oh, dear!" cried Miss Lilly as she struggled to stand up. "I'm afraid I've hurt my ankle."

Angelina knelt beside her teacher. "I'm so sorry, Miss Lilly," she whispered. Angelina felt terrible!

Now that Miss Lilly couldn't dance, Mr. Operatski wanted to cancel the Christmas ballet. Angelina found him at the theater, packing up his things.

"Please don't leave!" Angelina pleaded. "The show MUST go on—for Miss Lilly. And for the Queen. I'll dance the part of the Wicked Stepmouse. I can do it. I promise!"

Angelina convinced Mr. Operatski to stay. She called all the mouselings back to rehearsal. She even helped Henry learn to dance like a little beetle.

But secretly, Angelina was worried. She hadn't had time to practice her own part. Could she really do it?

On Christmas Eve, the Theater Royal was packed full. Angelina peeked nervously at the audience. She saw Mr. Operatski sitting beside Queen Seraphina, and just beside the Queen was . . . Miss Lilly!

Angelina's heart leaped, and she danced into the spotlight. She flung her arms above her head and began singing in a loud, wicked voice.

At first, the audience booed the Wicked Stepmouse, but by the end of her performance, the audience cheered and applauded. "Bravo!" called Mr. Operatski as Angelina danced off the stage and the red curtain came down.

On Christmas morning, Angelina stood before a very large present. "Go on," urged Mr. Mouseling. "Open it!"

Angelina ripped off the wrapping paper, and there was a toy theater like the one she had seen in the toy shop window. But this one was better, because Mr. Mouseling had made it to look exactly like the Theater Royal!

"It's beautiful!" cried Angelina as she hugged her father.

And now it was Angelina's turn to give a gift.

Angelina held out the Wicked Stepmouse's crown for Miss Lilly, who was celebrating with the Mouselings. "Thank you for making this the best Christmas ever!" said Angelina.

"For me?" Miss Lilly said warmly. "Oh! Merry Christmas, my darling Angelina."